Blueberry and Jam
Adventures in Maine

By Elizabeth Hamilton-Guarino

Illustrated by
Irina Prisacaru

Book Cover by: Irina Prisacaru

Illustrations by: Irina Prisacaru

ISBN: 9798872500667

1st edition 2023.

This Book Belongs to:

_____

Blueberry was no ordinary cat. He was a curious Maine Coon cat who lived in an old, weathered barn just outside of York. He got his name from his love of blueberries and the trail of blue paw prints he always left behind after snacking on the delicious berry.

Since Blueberry was a kitten,
he had always dreamed of being
an explorer and traveling the world.

One day, while sitting at their pine kitchen table, Blueberry announced, "Before traveling the world, I've decided I want to first see the sights in Maine. I want to explore my home state!"

"What a lovely idea, Blueberry!" Mama and Papa said. "There's no better place to start than right here in Maine!"

In preparation for his trip, Blueberry packed his suitcase full of clothes for his adventure. "Don't forget to put your camera, compass, and binoculars in your backpack too. Those will surely be useful along the way," his sister Rose said.

Blueberry and his best friend Jam bundled up a family photo, one of Blueberry's beloved books, and Jam's stuffed moose, Casco.

Mama baked them homemade blueberry tarts then packed a cooler of fresh milk and cheese from the farm and added them to the bundle.

13

After milking the cows, Papa fixed up his old, trusted truck to loan to Blueberry and Jam as a surprise.

"Here you go!" Papa said as he presented the truck to them. "Your very own exploring mobile!" Blueberry and Jam could not believe their eyes. They thanked him from whisker to whisker.

Early the next morning, Blueberry and Jam set out for their big adventure! As they drove off down the long, winding driveway, they could hear everyone from the farm calling out. "Goodbye, Blueberry and Jam. We'll miss you. We'll see you again soon. Have fun!"

The first stop on their journey was Kittery. At the Trading Post, Blueberry and Jam shopped for new swimsuits, boogie boards, and fishing poles. They could not wait to head up the coast to Old Orchard Beach.

19

At the beach, they loved riding the waves to shore. Blueberry and Jam looked for shells and sand dollars on the beach. It was quite a day!

The next day, Blueberry and Jam hopped back in their truck and headed for the Portland Head Light in Cape Elizabeth. They learned that the beautiful lighthouse was commissioned by President George Washington in 1791.

From Cape Elizabeth,
Blueberry and
Jam crossed the bridge
to Portland.

They walked the old cobblestone streets, looked at the old brick buildings, climbed the Portland Observatory, and ate ice cream cones on the wharf before driving up Route 1 to Freeport.

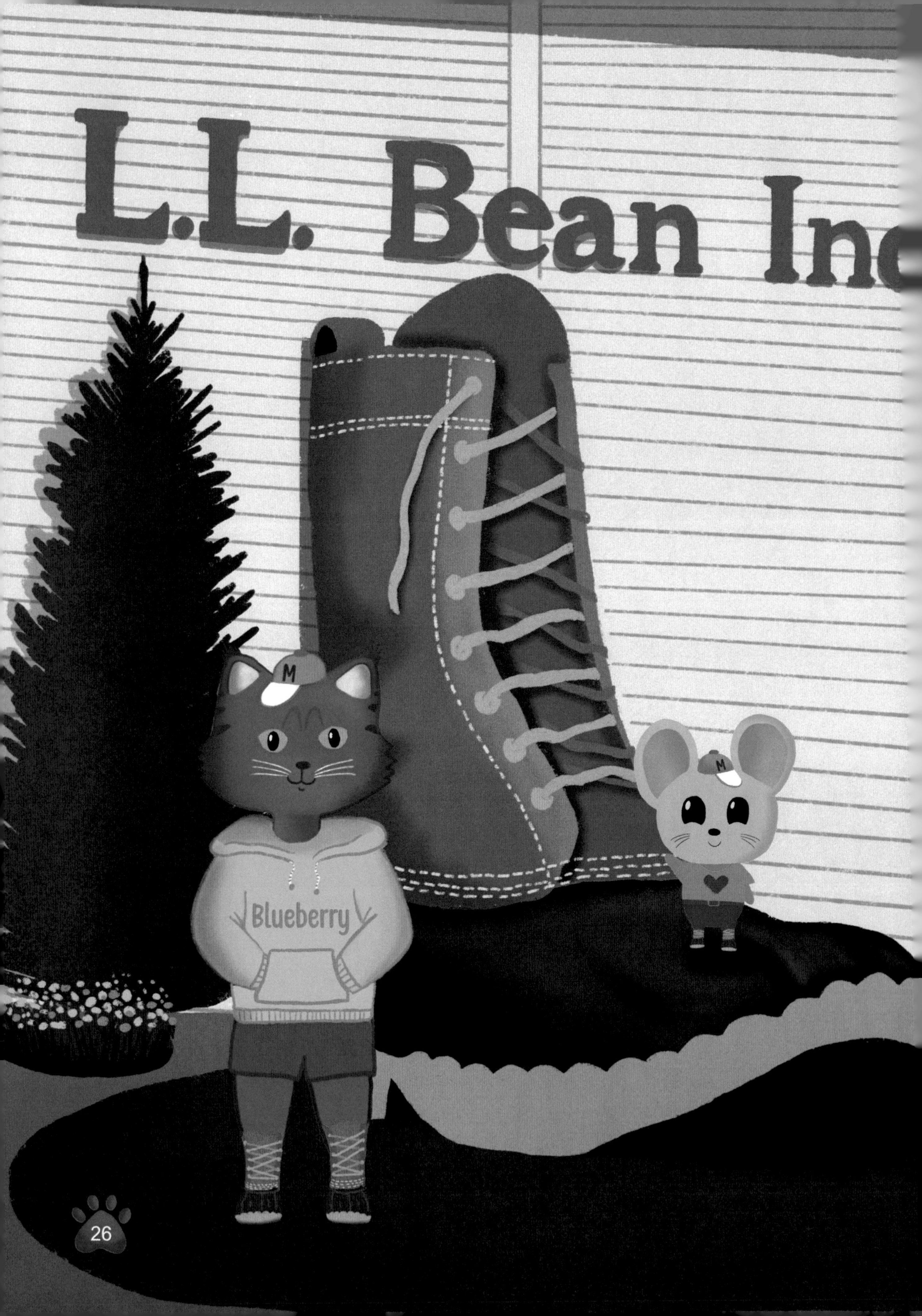
L.L. Bean Inc
Blueberry
M
M

In Freeport, they shopped for Maine coffee mugs, new hiking boots, and ate lobster rolls for lunch.

After a wonderful day exploring Freeport and the shops there, Blueberry and Jam drove further up Route 1. They crossed the Sagadahoc Bridge, next to the old Carlton Bridge, overlooking the shipyards in Bath and finally made their way to Boothbay Harbor.

In the morning, they stopped at the beautiful Coastal Maine Botanical Gardens in Boothbay.

They visited the magical Troll, Roskva, made by the artist Thomas Dambo. They learned the secret of Guardians of the Seeds by visiting all five Trolls.

That afternoon, Blueberry and Jam got to visit Papa's favorite sea captain, Captain Rusty.

CASEY ANNE

They had a great day on the boat! Blueberry and Jam learned all about lobster fishing and thought how wonderful it would be to eat lobster every day.

Blueberry and Jam took a delicious blueberry break at Pemaquid Point next. They climbed the lighthouse, looked out over the blue ocean and took pictures of the Monarch butterflies fluttering on the branches and floating in the crisp sea air.

They settled later that night in Camden at a small inn and relaxed by the fire.

During their stay, they hiked to the top of Mt. Battie for a panoramic view of Camden Harbor and Penobscot Bay and the quaint town of Camden below.

Blueberry and Jam loved all the sites on the Midcoast of Maine! The colors were so vivid and fresh!

In nearby Rockport, they went sailing on a windjammer cruise, marveling at the rocky islands off the coast.

Next, they drove to Bar Harbor and
Acadia National Park.

Acadia
National Park

They wanted to be at the top of Cadillac Mountain before sunrise. Blueberry had read that this is the first place in the United States where you can see the sunrise each day.

Slowly, the sun rose from the ocean into the sky and then became brilliant shades of red, yellow, and orange. It was breathtaking!

After a long cat and mouse nap, Blueberry and Jam biked the famous trails in Acadia. After, they relaxed by Jordan Pond with delicious hot chocolate and world-famous popovers.

The next day the ocean breeze was perfect for Acadia's big attraction, Thunder Hole! Water splashed everywhere with crashing thunder from the waves! Blueberry and Jam dressed in their boots and rain ponchos so they wouldn't get wet! Blueberry took a lot of pictures.

It was a short drive to Sand Beach, where they sat on the shore mesmerized by waves hitting the huge pink granite rocks and cliffs, while listening to the seagulls flying above.

Blueberry and Jam wanted to stay in the tranquility of the area forever, but they knew there was more exploring to do!

They drove to Machias in Downeast Maine through miles of blueberry fields and stopped to snack on the wild blueberries along the side of the road. They couldn't believe their eyes! Fields of wild blueberries as far as the eye could see.

With as many blueberries as they could ever wish for, Blueberry and Jam set their course for Grand Lake Stream. Before they left, Papa's friend Bruce had told them all about the world-famous fly-fishing there.

Early the next morning, Blueberry and Jam went fly-fishing for Landlocked Salmon. They learned that since 1903 only fly-fishing was allowed at Grand Lake Stream and that it has some of the best fly-fishing in the world.

In the afternoon, they stopped and had lunch at the Pine Tree Store.

49

Each night Blueberry and Jam wrote in their journals about their adventures. They wanted to remember every minute of their trip. Blueberry made a note that he wanted to explore Canada someday. For now, they headed to Baxter State Park in hopes of seeing moose, deer and maybe even a black bear or two.

When they arrived at Baxter State Park, they set up camp in the campground and packed for a hike. With their backpacks filled with their belongings and a trusted trail guide, Blueberry and Jam headed to the Appalachian Trail to climb Mt. Katahdin.

KATAHDIN

BAXTER PEAK   ELEVATION 5267 FT

NORTHERN TERMINUS OF THE
APPALACHIAN TRAIL

→ PAMOLA PEAK via KNIFE EDGE   1.1 M
↑ CHIMNEY POND CAMP GROUND via SADDLE   2.2
↑ ROARING BROOK CAMP GROUND via SADDLE   5.5
← KATAHDIN STREAM CAMP GROUND   5.5
← ABOL CAMP GROUND   4.4
← SPRINGER MOUNTAIN, GEORGIA via the A.T. 2.189.1

BAXTER STATE PARK

At the top of Baxter Peak, they met a fellow hiker who had been hiking for six months. He told Blueberry and Jam about his 2160-mile journey from Springer Mountain in Georgia to Katahdin. They shook hands and took a photo together.

Their next stop was in Greenville by Moosehead Lake. They camped with some friends they met along the way. Blueberry and Jam discovered they loved to camp, fish, eat s'mores, and relax around the campfire at night, telling stories of their daily expeditions.

Blueberry and Jam took a boat ride on Moosehead Lake, where they learned it is the largest lake in the Eastern United States.

They saw Mt. Kineo, which someone said looked like Half Dome in California. They noted that they might need to go see Yosemite someday.

While traveling from Greenville to Rockwood, Blueberry and Jam finally met a moose in a bog at sunset. As they shared their blueberries, the moose shared many interesting facts.

Blueberry and Jam learned that moose don't have front teeth and that only males have antlers. The moose also warned them to be careful driving at night because his moose friends are hard to see in the road. Blueberry took the moose's advice and drove carefully as he and Jam headed for Jackman and then on to Rangeley.

Blueberry's adventures took him and Jam through several small towns that surround the scenic Belgrade Lakes and then to Sugarloaf, one of Maine's famous ski mountains.

They stopped at a farm stand, bought some fresh vegetables, bread and blueberries for lunch, and then found a picnic area by a dairy farm.

They were tired from the long day of exploring so they got a great night's sleep! In the morning they drove to Augusta, the state capitol.

There, Blueberry and Jam took a guided tour of the Maine State House and the Maine State Museum. They learned even more about Maine in the museum, where they bought a few souvenirs to bring home.

65

Blueberry and Jam went south to go home, but first stopped at a fishing spot on Sebago Lake, where they each caught a string of trout for dinner. They saw deer and a flock of turkeys feeding in a hay field on the water's edge. He and Jam went for one more adventure - swimming in the lake before they headed home.

At dusk, Blueberry and Jam arrived back home in York. Mama, Papa, and Rose greeted them. Blueberry said, "It is so good to be home. We have so much to tell you. Maine is one big Vacationland!"

That night as they ate their fish dinner with blueberry muffins and whoopie pies for dessert, Blueberry told his family about the trip. He read from his journal and showed them pictures.

Gardens in Boothbay

Baxter Peak

Camden Hills

Cobblestone Streets

Trails in Acadia

Blueberry field

Freeport

Sebago Lake

Greenville

69

Blueberry and Jam fell asleep that night dreaming of their next adventure and of course…blueberries…

70

**The end, but not the end
of Blueberry and Jam's adventures!**

Did you know?

The Maine State Berry is the Wild Blueberry.

Blueberries in Maine are "low bush", also known as wild blueberries.

Maine produces about 98% or more of all the blueberries in the country, making it the single largest producer of blueberries in the United States. This fruit has become one of Maine's largest exports.

Blueberry plants are plentiful in Maine because their hardy nature allows them to withstand the harsh weather and rough soil that are common in the rural parts of Maine.

Blueberries are a great source of manganese, vitamin B6, vitamin C, vitamin K, and dietary fiber.

Wild blueberries are harvested from late July to early September in Maine. Harvesting is still mainly by hand rake. These hand rakes were invented over 100 years ago by Abijah Tabbut in Columbia Falls, Maine.

Notes

Notes